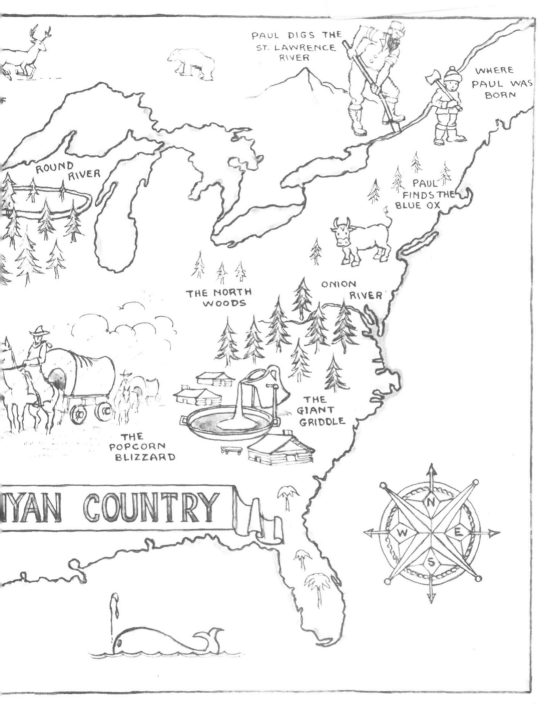

PAUL DIGS THE ST. LAWRENCE RIVER

WHERE PAUL WAS BORN

ROUND RIVER

PAUL FINDS THE BLUE OX

THE NORTH WOODS

ONION RIVER

THE POPCORN BLIZZARD

THE GIANT GRIDDLE

...YAN COUNTRY

Paul Bunyan Swings His Axe

PAUL BUNYAN
Swings His Axe

By Dell J. McCormick
Illustrated by the Author

19  97

THE CAXTON PRINTERS, LTD.
CALDWELL, IDAHO

First printing, November, 1936
Second printing, July, 1937
Third printing, November, 1937
Fourth printing, March, 1939
Fifth printing, June, 1940
Sixth printing, February, 1941
Seventh printing, October, 1941
Eighth printing, October, 1942
Ninth printing, February, 1944
Tenth printing, November, 1944
Eleventh printing, August, 1946
Twelfth printing, April, 1948
Thirteenth printing, September, 1950
Fourteenth printing, October, 1952
Fifteenth printing, January, 1955
Sixteenth printing, June, 1957
Seventeenth printing, June, 1960
Eighteenth printing, September, 1962
Nineteenth printing, May, 1964
Twentieth printing, December, 1964
Twenty-First printing, December, 1966
Twenty-Second printing, January, 1968
Twenty-Third printing, February, 1970
Twenty-Fourth printing, August, 1972
Twenty-Fifth printing, January, 1977
Twenty-Sixth printing, February, 1981
Twenty-Seventh printing, February, 1987
Twenty-Eighth printing, December, 1990
Twenty-Ninth printing, June, 1997

To Scotty MacDougall
Paul Bunyan's Pal

The Legend of

Paul Bunyan

*T*HESE stories of America's own legend are written for children from the authentic tales as told in lumber camps from Maine to California.

Students of folklore and legend recognize Paul Bunyan as one of America's few myths. The tales were originated by camp storytellers on long winter evenings and have been handed down for many generations with various embellishments.

The exact origin of Paul Bunyan is unknown. Some authorities trace the legends to eastern Canada, but it is generally believed that Maine heard the first Paul Bunyan story nearly one hundred years ago.

It is the hope of the author that this book for children will serve to perpetuate the stories of America's famous legend of the North Woods.

Stories

Paul Bunyan Swings His Axe

Paul Bunyan and His Boyhood

*M*ANY TALES are told of Paul Bunyan the giant woodsman. Mightiest hero of the North Woods! A man of great size and strength who was taller than the trees of the forest. He had such strength in his huge arms that they say he could take the tallest pine tree and break it in two with his bare hands. They tell of his mighty deeds and strange adventures from Maine to California.

He could outrun the swiftest deer, and cross the widest river in one great stride! Even today lumberjacks who work in the woods find small lakes and point them out, saying:

"Those are the footprints of Paul Bunyan that have been filled with water."

A giant logger was Paul and he chopped down whole forests in a single day. And he and his woodsmen logged off North Dakota in a single month! His axe was as wide as a barn door and had a great oak tree for a handle. It took six full-grown men to lift it!

They say that he was born in Maine and even as a baby he was so large that his mother and father had to have fourteen cows to supply milk for his porridge. Every morning when they looked at him he had grown two feet taller. They built a huge cradle for Paul and floated it in the ocean off the coast of Maine. The ocean waves would rock him to sleep.

One day he started bouncing up and down in his cradle and started a seventy-foot tidal wave that washed away towns and villages. After that Paul's folks gave up the idea of a floating cradle and took Paul with them into the Maine woods. Here they felt he could be kept out of mischief.

Paul spent his boyhood in the woods and helped his father cut down trees. They sawed the trees into logs and tied them together into large rafts which were floated down the river to the sawmills. Even as a boy he had the strength of twelve men and could ride a raft through the wildest rapids in the river.

One day the man at the sawmill refused to buy the logs. They were too large for his mill to cut up into lumber. So Paul chained them together again and pulled the raft back up the river to his father's camp. Imagine his dad's surprise to see young Paul wading up the river towing the great raft of logs behind him!

Everybody liked young Paul, and for miles around they told of his great feats of strength: of how he took an iron crowbar and bent it into a safety pin to hold together a rip in his trousers; of how at another time he came to the end of the field he was plowing with two oxen and having no room to turn the plow and oxen around, picked up the plow, oxen and all, and turned them around to start back the other way.

Yet Paul never boasted. When people asked him how strong he was he just laughed. And when Paul laughed the folks in the villages ran into their houses and hid in the cellars, thinking it was a thunderstorm!

In spite of his huge size, Paul was as quick as lightning. They say he was the only man in the woods who could blow out a candle at night and hop into bed before it was dark.

Being so quick on his feet was once his undoing. He was out in the woods hunting one day and shot at a bear. Paul was anxious to see if he had hit, and ran lickety-split toward it, only to get there before the shot he had fired.

15

The result was that he received a full load of his own buckshot in the seat of his breeches.

When Paul was full grown he decided he wanted to become the greatest lumberjack in America and perform great feats of logging. He dreamed of leading his men through wondrous adventures in the great forests of the West.

Babe the Blue Ox

*O*NE DAY when Paul was working in his father's logging camp in the Maine woods it started to snow. Day after day the soft fluffy snowflakes fell until the entire camp was covered with a blanket of snow. Log cabins disappeared from sight, and all but the tallest trees were buried under the great snowdrifts.

And the strangest thing of all was that the snow, instead of being white, was a bright sapphire blue! For miles and miles as far as one could see the forest was covered with beautiful blue snow. Loggers even today remember that year and call it the Winter of the Blue Snow.

When the snow had stopped falling, Paul put on his snowshoes and went out to find wood for his fireplace. As he was returning, he noticed two little ears sticking up through a snowdrift.

"It must be some poor animal lost and freezing to death," thought Paul. He reached down with one of his great hands and scooped the little thing out of the snow. It was a baby ox calf with thin wobbly legs. Paul put the little calf inside one of his large pockets and took him home. Soon he was curled up in front of the fireplace and as happy and warm as could be.

"Poor little baby!" said Paul as the little calf drank some warm milk and gratefully caressed Paul's hand with his tongue. Paul decided to call the little calf "Babe" and to keep him for a pet.

The strangest thing about Babe was that, even after he became thawed out, his coat remained a soft glossy blue. Paul nursed his new pet back to health, but his color never changed. The Winter of the Blue Snow had colored him blue, and blue he remained forever after.

Babe followed Paul wherever he went and grew larger each day. Every time Paul looked around the little calf seemed to have grown a foot taller.

In the spring, Paul built a little barn for Babe and put the calf inside for the night. The next morning, the barn was gone and so was the little blue calf. Paul searched high and low. Finally he found Babe calmly eating grass in a neighboring valley—with the barn perched right up on his back! He had outgrown it in a single night!

Paul became very fond of Babe and took him on all his adventures in the woods. He grew by leaps and bounds and soon was almost as large as Paul himself. Woodsmen tell us that when Babe was full grown he measured forty-two axe-handles between the eyes.

His appetite was tremendous. Every evening he ate a ton and a half of hay. Even then he wouldn't be satisfied to go to bed unless he had three wagonloads of turnips for dessert.

Paul taught him to help with the logging in the woods, and would give him an eighty-pound lump of sugar if he had been a good ox during the day. Babe was always full of mischief, however. He liked to roar and stamp his feet at night so the men would run out of the bunk-houses where they slept, thinking it was an earthquake! When Paul scolded him for it, Babe only chuckled to himself and pretended he was asleep.

Once when Babe was standing beside the cookhouse he winked at Paul and put his head in the cookhouse window. Babe gave a great sneeze and blew a whole barrel of flour over Hot

Biscuit Slim, the cook, and his helper, Cream Puff Fatty!

Babe was very useful in many ways. For instance, Paul had a lot of trouble with the crooked, twisting road that wound in and out through the forest. He finally tied one end of the road to a large stump and hitched Babe to the other end with a large logging chain. Babe dug his great hoofs in the ground and strained and tugged until he had pulled the entire road out straight. It was a mighty feat of strength. In doing it, he stretched the heavy iron links of the logging chain until it was a single iron bar!

During his first summer, Babe became fat and lazy and one day refused to pull the logs down the road to the river. He wanted to wait until winter when the snow was on the ground and logs would slide easier. Paul didn't say a word, but that night he had the men secretly whitewash the road. The next morning, Babe thought it was snow and pulled the logs without further trouble.

When winter finally came again and covered the Maine woods with beautiful white snow, Babe was the happiest ox in the world. He loved to roam through the woods on the new snowshoes that Paul had given him for his first birthday. The greatest trouble Paul had that winter was finding enough food for Babe, who was getting thin. One day he thought of a great idea and called Ole the big Swede. Ole was the camp blacksmith, and next to Paul, the largest man in camp.

"Ole," he said, "I want you to make the largest pair of green eyeglasses in the world." When Ole finished, Paul put the glasses on Babe, strapping them over his nose. He then turned Babe out in the snow again. To Babe, with his new green glasses, all the snow looked like nice green grass! He ate and ate and grew fat and healthy again in no time at all.

In all the woods, there was no one so kindly toward Babe as Paul Bunyan, and no ox was ever as faithful to its master as Babe, the famous Blue Ox.

Paul Bunyan's Camp on Onion River

*O*NE DAY Paul's father was offered a contract to log the Onion River Country, which was in the mountains to the west. It was wild and mountainous, and his father refused. Paul spoke up:

"Father, I am no longer a boy. I want to become the world's champion logger. With the help of your men and Babe the Blue Ox, I will log the Onion River Country and start a camp of my own."

His father agreed, and Paul gathered a crew of the finest lumberjacks in the land. He promised them many fine adventures if they would follow him into the new country.

They gathered their axes and saws and loaded the wagons. Paul had Ole the Blacksmith put wheels under the kitchen and dining room and even under the bunkhouses where the men slept at night. Paul tied them together with

25

strong logging chains, and Babe the Blue Ox pulled the camp houses after him as if they had been so many toothpicks.

When they arrived, the first thing Paul set out to do was to build the largest logging camp in the world. People for miles around came to see it when it was finished. It was so big that when it was breakfast time in the kitchen, it was dinnertime in the blacksmith shop at the other end of the camp.

Every day more men joined the camp of Paul Bunyan. Finally, there were so many that Paul had them work in three shifts: one group working in the woods, one going and coming from the woods, and a third at camp, eating.

Paul bought a great watch so that everybody would know when it was mealtime. It was four feet across the face and tied to his trousers pocket with a logging chain. Of course it cost a lot of money, but Paul said it gained enough time in the first three days to pay for itself. At dinnertime Hot Biscuit Slim would blow a huge dinner horn. It was so large and made such a noise that he knocked down two hundred trees and started a windstorm on the Gulf of Mexico. After that, they decided not to use it. Later, they sold it, and the tin was used to put a new roof on the Capitol at Washington.

It was a very busy camp. Hundreds of men, called swampers, cut paths through the woods. Then the sawyers came and sawed the trees down. As the trees fell, you could hear the men shouting, "Timber!! Timber-r-r!!" to warn the others. Another crew cut the trees up into logs. Then Babe the Blue Ox pulled them down to the river where they were left until spring and then floated down the river in great rafts to the waiting sawmills.

Paul Bunyan finally invented the double-bitted axe with a blade on each side so his men could work twice as fast. Paul himself cut down the largest trees. Sometimes he chopped so fast his axe became red-hot and had to be dipped into a lake of cold water every five minutes to cool it off.

Ole the Big Swede proved to be the best blacksmith on Onion River. When he started to shoe a horse, he would take the animal right up into his lap like a baby. Then he would turn the horse on its back and nail the shoes on. He never took more than ten minutes to shoe a horse.

He once made a set of great iron shoes for Babe the Blue Ox. They were the largest shoes in the world. They were so heavy that when Ole carried one of them from the blacksmith shop he sank two feet in solid rock at every step!

Day by day the camp covered more ground until the men had to take a week's food with them when they walked from one end of it to the other. Even the smokestack on the kitchen was so high they had to have it hinged in the middle to let the clouds go by. The dining room tables were two miles long, and the cookhouse boys wore roller skates so they could serve the food quickly.

Everything was on a huge scale. Even the crumbs that fell on the floor were so large that the chipmunks who ate them grew as large as wolves. They chased all the bears out of the country. Later the settlers who came shot them for tigers! Every morning after breakfast it took a crew of thirty men to dispose of the egg-shells, coffee grounds, and prune pits that were piled outside the cookhouse window.

Finally, all the logs were cut and floated down the Onion River to the mills, and Paul decided to move on into a new country which lay directly to the west. The new country was later known as the Red River Valley.

Hot Biscuit Slim and Cream Puff Fatty

*T*HE RED River got its name from Paul's camp. It seems one of Paul's cookhouse boys drove a ketchup wagon in the dining room. Every meal the men ate so much ketchup that the boy would only get halfway around when his wagon would be empty.

This made him so angry that one day he tipped the ketchup wagon over and left camp. The ketchup ran down into the river and colored the water red, and to this day that part of the country is known as the Red River Valley.

When Paul moved his camp into the new country, he found that the dining room was still too small for all his men. Every day dinner would be from two to three hours late. Paul was angry and shouted, "Hot Biscuit Slim!" Three men who were standing beside him were blown over by the force of his voice. They rolled over and over and lit on their feet running and never stopped until they were well out of the reach of his voice.

Hot Biscuit Slim, the cook, came on the run. Paul said, "I want a larger kitchen where two hundred cooks can work at the same time. Also build a larger dining room. Make the tables six miles long! Yesterday the men sat down to dinner and it was lunch time the next day before the food arrived. By that time the biscuits were cold, and who wants cold biscuits?"

So they cleared the forests for miles around and built a huge kitchen and dining room. The blacksmith, Ole the Swede, made a huge black kettle. It held eleven hundred gallons of soup.

When Hot Biscuit Slim made soup he rowed out into the center of the kettle with boatloads of cabbages, turnips, and potatoes, and shoveled them into the boiling hot water. In a few hours they had wonderful vegetable soup.

Next the blacksmith made a ten-acre griddle pan for hot cakes. Hot Biscuit Slim strapped flat sides of bacon on the feet of the cookhouse boys. They skated back and forth over the huge griddle until it was well greased.

They thought it was great fun and played tag and crack the whip. The griddle was hot, and they sometimes fell and burned their trousers. When the griddle began to steam it became so foggy no one could see across it.

Every Sunday morning for breakfast Paul's campers had hot griddle cakes. They were so large it took five men to eat one. Paul himself ate twelve or fourteen. The cookhouse boys worked all day Saturday mixing dough and bringing in huge barrels of maple syrup.

Sunday dinner, however, was the biggest meal of the week. Hot Biscuit Slim would cook the very best soup, the finest vegetables, and the nicest spring chickens.

One Saturday he said to Ole the Big Swede, "Tomorrow, I am going to have the best Sunday dinner of the year. When the men are through eating my hot biscuits with jelly, spinach, cucumbers, young red radishes, and chicken pie, they won't be able to eat a mouthful of dessert."

Cream Puff Fatty, who made the desserts, overheard this. He was very angry, for his pride was hurt. "So Hot Biscuit Slim thinks they won't eat any dessert. We shall see!" said he.

Cream Puff Fatty called the dessert boys together and said, "We will make cream puffs that will melt in your mouth! Light creamy ones with whipped cream a foot high! We shall see if they refuse to eat dessert!"

The dinner hour arrived. The men sat down and started to eat. Soup, vegetables, and salads disappeared as the men ate and ate. When the chicken pie arrived, they were almost full.

"Oh look! Chicken pie!" they shouted. They ate the chicken pie. Then the cookhouse boys on roller skates brought in more large platters of food.

"Hot biscuits and jelly! Hurrah!" they cried. They ate the biscuits and there didn't seem to be room for another mouthful of food. Cream Puff Fatty was in despair. He looked down the long dining room. The men were almost finished. It looked as if they couldn't eat another mouthful.

"Now is the time, boys!" cried Cream Puff Fatty. The dessert boys strapped on their roller skates and started down the long tables.

"Cream puffs! Cream puffs!" the men shouted as they saw large plates of fluffy white cakes topped with whipped cream. With a shout they picked up their forks and started eating again. Not a man left the dining room! Every single cream puff was eaten!

"Three cheers for Cream Puff Fatty!" yelled the men. The fat little dessert cook had tears of

joy in his eyes. "It was a wonderful dinner!"
said Cream Puff Fatty as he shook hands with
Hot Biscuit Slim.

The Mysterious Round River

WHEN Paul Bunyan had cut down all the trees in the Red River Country, he called his men together.

"Tomorrow we go into the North Woods where no white man has ever gone before. It is to the west and north near the Great Lakes. And it is the largest forest in the world. The Indians say that the trees grow so large it takes all afternoon to walk around one."

Tiny Tim, the water boy, clapped his hands, he was so excited.

"Do the trees grow taller than the pines on Onion River?" he asked Paul.

Paul Bunyan smiled.

"The trees there grow so tall that you can only see the tops of them on very clear days," he said, "and they grow so close together they hide the sun."

Everyone wanted to see this wonderful forest. So Paul hitched Babe the Blue Ox to the bunkhouse and the kitchen and all the rest of the camp houses and started on the long trip to the North Woods.

They followed an Indian trail through the forest for thirty days and thirty nights. Then they came to a large, deep river in the middle of the woods.

"Everybody stop! Here is our new camp," said Paul.

The force of Paul's voice knocked Ole the Big Swede over and broke eighteen windows in the dining room.

Babe the Blue Ox was thirsty and went to the river and drank and drank. The river became smaller and smaller, and all the fish were left high and dry on the banks. The cookhouse boys caught them with their bare hands. That evening Hot Biscuit Slim cooked a fine fish dinner.

The next day the river filled with water again, and the men started cutting down the trees and sawing them into logs.

In a few days the first raft was ready. Ole the Big Swede jumped on the raft. Twenty men followed him. They cut the ropes that held the raft to the shore.

"Hurrah! They're off!" cried the men on the bank as the logs started down the river.

The river wound in and out through the dark forest. Ole and his men saw bears and once in a while a deer that had come down to the river to drink.

Soon they came to an open space in the forest.

"Look ahead, men," said Ole. "We are almost out of the woods."

Here all the trees had been cut down. For miles along the river bank they saw nothing but tree stumps.

Suddenly one of the men cried:

"Look! There's a camp exactly like the camp of Paul Bunyan!"

The river quickly carried the raft of logs past the camp and down into some more woods.

A little later they came to another open space and another camp exactly like the camp of Paul Bunyan.

"This is queer," thought Ole the Big Swede, "for Paul told me we were the only woodsmen in the North Woods."

The men were getting frightened. Everyone kept looking ahead as the river carried them along through the dark forest. Little Blackie, an axeman, pointed ahead. Sure enough, there was another camp, and it too looked like the camp of Paul Bunyan!

There was a kitchen and a dining room and a bunkhouse and even a blacksmith shop painted red like the shop in the camp of Paul Bunyan.

As they went past this camp, Blackie pointed to a clothesline on the shore.

There is a blue shirt exactly like the one I hung on the line back in Paul's camp!"

Just before dark they came to another open space in the forest and another camp exactly like the camp of Paul Bunyan.

"Look at the men on the river bank waving at us," said Ole, "and see the huge giant walking out in the water."

The men on the raft were about to jump into the water and swim for their lives when little Blackie cried out:

"Why that is Paul Bunyan himself!"

And sure enough, it was Paul; and there on the bank they saw Hot Biscuit Slim and Tiny Tim and all their friends.

Paul took them to shore and they found out that they had been on the mysterious Round River that flowed around and around in a circle. They had been going by their own camp all the time!

The Winter of the Blue Snow

*O*NE NIGHT in the North Woods the men were seated around a campfire. They were telling of their adventures in other camps. Someone asked Paul to tell them of his earlier adventures.

"Tell us about the Winter of the Blue Snow," cried Tiny Tim.

"Well," said Paul, "I was logging with my father back in the Maine woods. That was the winter I found Babe the Blue Ox. Only he was a little calf then not much larger than Tiny Tim. Old-timers sometimes speak of it as the year of the two winters. When summer came, it got cold again, and in the fall it turned colder. For two solid years the snow covered the ground so deep that only the tops of the tallest trees showed through the snow.

"The snow was blue in color and over two hundred feet deep in places. The Great Lakes

43

froze solid to the very bottom and would never have thawed out if loggers hadn't cut the ice up into small blocks and set them out in the sun to melt. When spring finally came, they had to get a complete new set of fish for the lakes.

"The camp was buried under the snow, and the men rode up to the surface in elevators. Each man had sixteen blankets so that he would be warm at night. Shot Gunderson, who was head sawyer, can tell you how cold it was. He slept under forty-two blankets, and one morning he got lost and couldn't find his way out. It was three days before we could find him, and by that time he had almost starved to death.

"It was so cold that when Hot Biscuit Slim set the coffee out to cool it froze so fast the ice was hot. The men had to eat breakfast with their mittens on, and sometimes the hot biscuits were frozen solid before they could take a bite.

"The bunkhouses where we slept were so cold that the words froze as soon as the men spoke. The frozen words were thrown in a pile behind the stove, and the men would have to wait until the words thawed out before they knew what was being said. When the men sang, the music froze and the following spring the woods were full of music as odd bits of song gradually thawed out.

"Very few trees were cut that winter as we had to make holes in the snow and lower the men down to the trees. Then we would pull the trees out of the holes with long ropes.

"The men all let their beards grow long as a protection against the cold. Some of the beards were so long that they got in the way, and the men were always stumbling over them. So we made a new rule in the camp. Anyone with a beard over six feet long had to keep the end of it tucked in his boots. In the spring the beards were so thick the men had to shave them off with axes.

"When Christmas came that year the men were homesick for some good old-fashioned white snow. 'It doesn't seem like Christmas,' they cried, 'with all this bright blue snow on the ground.'

"So I decided to put on snowshoes and travel west until I could find some white snow. Well, sir, I climbed over mountains and across plains right out to the Pacific Ocean, which was frozen solid. The ice seemed fairly thick, so I kept on going. And do you know I had to travel clear to China before I could find any white snow!

But the men were certainly happy when I brought them back some white snow for Christmas!

"We had a lot of trouble with frost-biters that winter. They were little animals about three inches long that lived in the snow. They bit the men on the feet as they walked along. Even now, you hear of people being frostbitten, but that winter it was much more dangerous.

"The blue snow finally melted in the spring and filled many lakes in the woods. To this day, many of the beautiful lakes in the mountains are still colored blue from the Winter of the Blue Snow. The Indians called the country 'The Land of the Sky Blue Water.'"

Johnnie Inkslinger and His Magic Pen

*O*NE DAY a visitor asked Paul how many men were in the camp. Paul didn't know. There was Hot Biscuit Slim and his two hundred cooks. Ole the Big Swede, Blackie, Tiny Tim, and hundreds more.

Paul tried to count them one day at dinner, but they kept coming and going for hours. He asked Cream Puff Fatty how many desserts he had made. "Eight thousand," said Cream Puff Fatty.

"Good!" said Paul. "Then we must have eight thousand men."

"No," said Cream Puff Fatty, "because some of the men don't eat desserts, and Ole the Big Swede eats seven, except when it is strawberry shortcake. Then he eats ten."

So Paul gave up even trying to count the men and sent for Johnnie Inkslinger to do the arithmetic for the camp. Johnny Inkslinger was the best bookkeeper in the North Woods—a tall sad-looking man with a bald head. He always wore a large pair of eyeglasses perched at the end of his long, thin nose.

He added and subtracted and multiplied endless rows of figures day and night. He became the fastest bookkeeper in the world and never made a mistake. One night he counted all the stars in the sky and never missed one. Johnnie Inkslinger kept track of everything, even down to the last ear of corn in the kitchens.

His magic pen never ran out of ink. A long rubber hose connected it to a ten-gallon barrel of ink, and that is how the fountain pen was invented. Johnnie Inkslinger wrote so fast that the barrel of ink had to be filled every two days.

"You are using too much ink," said Paul one day. "We cannot buy it fast enough." So Johnnie Inkslinger thought of a plan. He quit dotting his "i's" and crossing his "t's" and from then on saved nine gallons of ink a week.

Johnnie Inkslinger invented new ways of adding and subtracting that are used to this day. He wrote every number down twice so as not to make a single mistake.

He also invented the mistake eraser. This was a large rubber sponge to be rubbed over a page of figures. It erased only the mistakes and left all the rest of the figures as they were. Johnnie finally had no use for it as he made no mistakes. He gave it to Hot Biscuit Slim.

Hot Biscuit Slim used it for awhile, but he never liked it. The magic sponge erased almost every figure he made. He gave it to Ole the Big Swede. Ole tried it just once and it erased the whole sheet of paper until there was only a blank space where all the figures had been. It seems Ole was very poor at arithmetic, and no matter how many times he added two and two it always came out six.

Johnnie Inkslinger once tried to figure out how much it cost to feed Babe the Blue Ox, but he finally had to give it up. Every time he added up the figures he found that Babe had eaten another barnful of hay. Then he would have to start all over again. This made him so angry that he told Paul he would quit doing arithmetic forever. Nevertheless, Johnnie Inkslinger remained with Paul during all his years of adventure in the woods.

The Strange Sickness of Babe the Blue Ox

THE BLUE OX was always a favorite around camp. In spite of his great size, he was always playing jokes on the men. One day Cream Puff Fatty was out fishing in a lake. Just for a joke Babe drank it dry while Fatty was rowing for shore. Imagine how silly the fat little cook looked trying to row a boat on dry land!

Finally, Paul hired Brimstone Bill to take care of Babe. Bill wasn't as tall as Ole the Big Swede, but he was wider than he was tall, and very strong and active for his age. He was well over sixty years old and could leap in the air and kick the ceiling with both feet. He had the hobnails on the soles of his shoes made to form his initials. Every time he kicked the ceiling of the bunkhouses he left his initials, B B, there and you can find marks of them there to this day.

Paul told him to try to keep Babe out of mischief. If left to himself, Babe would eat everything in sight. If Cream Puff Fatty put some pies out to cool, Babe would eat them all. He loved hot cakes best of all and could eat them faster than Hot Biscuit Slim and his cooks could make them for him on the kitchen stove. One day this fondness for hot cakes was the cause of trouble for Babe.

No one knew just how it happened, but Brimstone Bill noticed that Babe hardly touched his turnips at dinner one night. The next morning the Blue Ox groaned and rolled his eyes in pain.

"Babe is sick!" cried Brimstone Bill. "Somebody call Johnnie Inkslinger!" Johnnie was the only one in camp who knew how to cure sickness of any kind. He arrived in a few minutes with a suitcaseful of pills. Babe swallowed the pills, suitcase and all, but it didn't seem to do a bit of good.

"Open your mouth and say Ahaaaaaaaa!" said Johnnie Inkslinger.

Babe did as he was told.

"Just as I thought," said Johnnie, "His throat is all red and swollen!"

So they poured twenty-five barrels of cough medicine down his huge throat. It was no use.

Babe became sicker. Johnnie Inkslinger was desperate!

"We will lower six men down into his mouth with ropes to find the trouble," said he. He told the men to take lanterns along and explore every inch of the way and to keep on going until they found out the cause of the trouble.

Soon they had built a huge scaffold and lowered the men down into Babe's mouth. Down they went, past great white teeth, sliding and crawling down his rough tongue. They went down the huge passage that led to his stomach.

It grew dark. Johnnie Inkslinger led the way with his lantern. On and on they went until they came to the door at the entrance to Babe's stomach.

"Stay here, men," said Johnnie, "and I will crawl in and see if I can find anything!" In the center of the stomach was a great black object. Johnnie Inkslinger called the men and together they tied ropes around it. Then he gave three quick jerks on the rope, which was the signal for the men outside to pull them up again.

Babe, in his fondness for hot cakes, had become greedy. He had eaten the hot cakes, stove and all! The stove was hot and of course gave him indigestion.

In a few days, Babe was well again, but it was a great lesson to him. Never again did he put his head in the kitchen when the cooks were not around. From then on, he never ate another hot cake.

Paul Bunyan Digs the St. Lawrence River

*O*NE SUMMER Paul decided to leave the North Woods and go back to Maine to visit his father and mother. When he arrived, they talked about old times, and Paul asked about Billy Pilgrim, the biggest man in that part of the country.

"What is this Billy Pilgrim doing?" asked Paul.

"He is digging the St. Lawrence River between the United States and Canada," said Paul's father. "There was nothing to separate the two countries. People never knew when they were in the United States and when they were in Canada."

Paul Bunyan went to see Billy. He found that Billy Pilgrim and his men had been digging for three years and had dug only a very small ditch. Paul laughed when he saw it.

"My men could dig the St. Lawrence River in three weeks," said Paul.

This made Billy angry for he thought no one could dig a large river in three weeks.

"I will give you a million dollars if you can dig the St. Lawrence River in three weeks!" said Billy Pilgrim.

So Paul sent for Babe the Blue Ox, Ole the Big Swede, Brimstone Bill, and all his woodsmen.

Paul told Ole to make a huge scoop shovel as large as a house. They fastened it to Babe with a long buckskin rope. He hauled many tons of dirt every day and emptied the scoop shovel in Vermont. You can see the large piles of dirt there to this day. They are called the Green Mountains.

Every night Johnnie Inkslinger, who did the arithmetic, would take his large pencil and mark one day off the calendar on the wall.

Billy Pilgrim was afraid they would finish digging the river on time. He did not want to pay Paul Bunyan the million dollars, for at heart he was a miser. So he thought of a plan to prevent Paul from finishing the work.

One night Billy called his men together and said, "When everybody has gone to bed we will go out and pour water on the buckskin rope so it will stretch, and Babe the Blue Ox will not be able to pull a single shovelful of dirt!"

The next day, Babe started toward Vermont with the first load of dirt. When he arrived there, he looked around and the huge scoop shovel was nowhere to be seen. For miles and miles the buckskin rope had stretched through the forests and over the hills.

Babe didn't know what to do. He sat down and tried to think, but everyone knows an ox isn't very bright; so he just sat there. After a while the sun came out and dried the buckskin and it started to shrink to normal size.

Babe planted his large hoofs between two mountains and waited. The buckskin rope kept shrinking and shrinking. Soon the scoop shovel came into view over the hills. Then Babe emptied it and started back after another load.

In exactly three weeks the St. Lawrence River was all finished, but still Billy Pilgrim did not want to pay Paul the money.

"Very well," said Paul, "I will remove the water!" So he led Babe the Blue Ox down to the river, and Babe drank the St. Lawrence River dry.

Billy Pilgrim only chuckled to himself for he knew that the first rain would fill it again. Soon it began to rain, and the river became as large as ever.

So Paul picked up a large shovel.

"If you do not pay the money you owe me I will fill the river up again," said Paul.

He threw in a shovelful of dirt. He threw in another and another, but still Billy Pilgrim would not pay him the money.

"I will pay you half your money," said Billy.

Paul again picked up his shovel and tossed more dirt into the river.

"I will pay you two thirds of your money," said Billy.

Paul kept throwing more dirt into the river until he had thrown a thousand shovelfuls.

"Stop! I will pay you all your money!" cried Billy.

So Paul Bunyan was finally paid in full for digging the St. Lawrence River. The thousand shovelfuls of dirt are still there.

They are called the Thousand Islands.

Mirror Lake and the Black Duck Dinner

*W*HEN they broke up the camp on the St. Lawrence River, Paul told Hot Biscuit Slim to prepare a wonderful dinner. It was to be on Sunday, the last day in camp. Slim and his cooks were excited, as you can imagine.

For miles around the farmers brought in strawberries, peas, new potatoes, and gallons of rich cream, for Cream Puff Fatty to make into his famous cream puffs. The men cut fifty-five wagonloads of wood so the stoves could be kept burning until all the food was cooked.

"What kind of meat are we going to have for dinner today?" asked Paul. Hot Biscuit Slim hid his head in shame. Slim was the best cook in the woods, but somehow he always forgot something. Once he forgot to order milk. Another time he forgot to bake bread. This time he had entirely forgotten to order any meat for the dinner.

"I forgot to tell the butchers to bring any meat!" admitted Slim.

"No meat at all?" asked Paul.

"No meat!" cried Slim. "I forgot all about the meat!"

Johnnie Inkslinger heard them talking and called to Hot Biscuit Slim, "How would you like to give your men a nice black duck dinner?"

"Where will I be able to get the ducks?" asked Slim.

"Come with me!" said Johnnie.

They went to Paul's bunkhouse, and Johnnie Inkslinger pointed to the huge hand mirror that Paul used when he combed his large beard. It was one hundred and twenty feet from tip to tip. Next he told Brimstone Bill to harness sixteen teams of horses. With the aid of horses, they dragged the huge mirror through the woods to a near-by meadow.

They placed the mirror on the ground with the glass side up and piled dirt around the edges. In a short time the mirror looked like a beautiful little lake. The trees along the edge could be seen in the mirror as if it had been real water.

"Everybody go back to camp," said Johnnie Inkslinger, "and in an hour I will bring you all the black ducks you can possibly eat!"

When everybody had gone, he hid in some near-by bushes and, putting his hands to his mouth, he gave the call of the wild black ducks.

"Quack! Quack! Quack!" said Johnnie Inkslinger. Johnnie made a noise like a real duck, for he had lived all his life in the woods and knew the calls of all the wild animals.

The ducks swooped down and, mistaking the hard glass mirror for water, fell against it with a crash and were stunned. Johnnie soon had enough for dinner, and the wagons carried them back to camp.

"Here are enough ducks for a wonderful black duck dinner," he said to Hot Biscuit Slim as the wagons drove up to the kitchen. Hot Biscuit Slim was beside himself for joy! The cookhouse boys quickly plucked the feathers, and soon the ducks were merrily roasting in the huge ovens.

"We will have the best duck dinner that anyone has ever eaten," cried Hot Biscuit Slim, "and the finest roast duck of all will go to Johnnie Inkslinger!"

The Kingdom of North Dakota

S OON AFTER Paul had finished digging the St. Lawrence River he received a letter from the King of Sweden. It seems that the King had heard of Paul Bunyan through Ole the Big Swede. He wanted Paul to cut down all the trees in North Dakota so the Swedes could settle there and farm the land. The King wrote that he wanted this job done in one month so the farmers could plant their grain at once. All the trees were to be cut up and made into toothpicks for the Swedish army.

When this huge job was finished, all the Swedes in North America were to settle in the New Kingdom of North Dakota and farm the land. This was about the largest job that Paul ever attempted. He soon gathered his men together and started moving his camp to North Dakota. When they all arrived, he built the largest camp the world had ever seen.

The bunks in the new sleeping quarters were eighteen decks high and the men in the top bunks had to get up an hour earlier in the morning in order to get down to breakfast on time. The dining room was longer than ever, and the boy that drove the salt and pepper wagon around the tables would only be halfway around by nightfall. He would stay overnight at the other end and drive back the next day.

Paul had to finish the job in one month, so he hired the Seven Axemen. They were famous woodsmen and could cut down trees faster than anyone except Paul himself. They were all cousins, and each was named Frank. It was very confusing, because every time Paul shouted "Frank!" all the Seven Axemen would drop their work and run over to see what he wanted.

The Seven Axemen used great double-bitted axes that an ordinary man could not lift. When the axes became dull they would start a round, flat rock rolling down the hillside and run beside it holding the blades of their axes against the rock until they were sharp again.

No matter how fast they worked, the huge job was always being delayed. Paul began to have bad luck. First, Babe the Blue Ox lost his heavy iron shoes in a swamp, and a new mine had to be opened to get enough iron to make him a new set.

Next came the great fog that covered the earth like a blanket. It was so thick that the fish in the river couldn't tell where the water left off and the fog began. They swam around in the fog and got lost among the trees in the forest. When the fog disappeared, thousands of small fish were left in the woods many miles from the nearest stream.

The Seven Axemen had to chop a tunnel in the fog from the kitchen to the dining room so the cooks could serve food. The fog even got into the coffee and made it so weak the men wouldn't drink it. At night the men had to sleep with mosquito netting over their heads to keep the tadpoles from getting in their ears.

Finally the fog went away, but all the blankets and shirts were so wet it took fourteen days to dry them out.

At last all the trees were cut down and split into toothpicks, but still the King of Sweden wasn't satisfied. He wrote Paul another letter which said, "My farmers will not be able to till the soil with all the stumps," and the farmers refused to settle in the new Kingdom of North Dakota.

Paul called Johnnie Inkslinger into the office and said, "You are good at solving problems. What are we going to do about the stumps?" Johnnie Inkslinger thought and thought for seven days and nights.

"We will send for several large fire hoses and flood the ground with water," said Johnnie Inkslinger finally. "Babe the Blue Ox, as you all know, doesn't like to get his feet wet, for that gives him a cold in the head.

"With water all over the ground, he will walk on the stumps. He is so heavy his huge hoofs will drive the stumps into the ground."

The men did as Johnnie said. They covered the whole country with water. Babe roamed all over North Dakota, stepping very carefully from stump to stump to avoid getting his feet wet. His heavy weight drove the stumps six feet under ground.

The King of Sweden was finally satisfied, and to this day there isn't a single tree or stump in the whole state of North Dakota.

The Popcorn Blizzard

WHEN Paul Bunyan had cut down all the trees in North Dakota, he decided to go west. It was summertime, and the forest was sweet with the smell of green trees. The spreading branches cast their cool shadows on the ground.

"We must cross vast plains," said Paul to his men, "where it is so hot that not even a blade of grass can grow. You must not become too thirsty as there will be very little water to drink."

Paul knew it would be a long, hard journey, so he decided to send all the heavy camp equipment by boat down the Mississippi River and around the Horn to the Pacific Ocean. Paul told Billy Whiskers, a little bald-headed logger with a bushy beard, to take a crew of men and build a boat. Billy had once been a sailor. In a short time the boat was finished and loaded with all the heavy camp tools.

Everyone cheered as Billy Whiskers and his men started down the Mississippi River on their long trip. Billy wore an admiral's hat and looked every inch the sailor, although he hadn't been on board a ship for thirty-five years.

With Paul and Babe the Blue Ox leading the way, the rest of the camp then started across the plains on their long journey west. In a few days they had left the woods and were knee deep in sand that stretched out before them for miles and miles. The sun became hotter and hotter!

"I made some vanilla ice-cream," said Hot Biscuit Slim one day as he gave the men their lunch, "but the ice became so hot under this boiling sun that I couldn't touch it!"

Tiny Tim, the water boy, was so hot and tired that Paul had to put him up on Babe's back where he rode the rest of the trip. Every time Babe took a step forward, he moved ahead two miles, and Tiny Tim had to hold on with all his might. Even Ole the Big Swede, who was so strong he could carry a full-grown horse under each arm, began to tire.

There was not a tree in sight. Paul Bunyan's

men had never before been away from the forest. They missed the cool shade of the trees. Whenever Paul stopped to rest, thirty or forty men would stand in his shadow to escape the boiling sun.

"I won't be able to last another day," cried Brimstone Bill, "if it doesn't begin to cool off soon!"

Even Paul Bunyan became tired finally and took his heavy double-bitted axe from his shoulder and dragged it behind him as he walked. The huge axe cut a ragged ditch through the sand that can be seen to this day. It is now called the Grand Canyon, and the Colorado River runs through it.

It became so hot that the men were exhausted and refused to go another step. Hot Biscuit Slim had complained that there was very little food left in camp. That night Paul took Babe the Blue Ox and went on alone into the mountains to the north. In the mountains Paul found a farmer with a barnful of corn.

"I will buy your corn," said Paul to the farmer. So he loaded all the corn on Babe's back and started for camp. By the time he arrived there, the sun was shining again and the day grew hotter as the sun arose overhead. Soon it became so hot that the corn started popping. It shot up into the air in vast clouds of white puffy popcorn.

It kept popping and popping and soon the air was filled with wonderful white popcorn. It came down all over the camp and almost covered the kitchen. The ground became white with popcorn as far as the eye could see. It fell like a snowstorm until everything was covered two feet deep with fluffy popcorn.

"A snowstorm! A snowstorm!" cried the men as they saw it falling. Never had they seen anything like it before. Some ran into the bunkhouses and put on their mittens and others put on heavy overcoats and woolen caps. They clapped each other on the back and laughed and shouted for joy.

"Let's make snowshoes!" cried Ole the Big Swede. So they all made snowshoes and waded around in the white popcorn and threw popcorn snowballs at each other, and everybody forgot how hot it had been the day before. Even the horses thought it was real snow, and some of them almost froze to death before the men could put woolen blankets on them and lead them to shelter.

Babe the Blue Ox knew it was only popcorn and winked at Paul.

Paul Bunyan chuckled to himself at the popcorn blizzard and decided to start west again while the men were feeling so happy. He found them all huddled around the kitchen fire.

"Now is the time to move on west," said Paul, "before it begins to get hot again." So they packed up and started. The men waded through the popcorn and blew on their hands to keep them warm. Some claimed their feet were frostbitten, and others rubbed their ears to keep them from freezing.

After traveling for a few weeks more, they saw ahead of them the great forest they had set out to reach. They cheered Paul Bunyan who had led them safely over the hot desert plains. Babe the Blue Ox laughed and winked at Paul whenever anyone mentioned the great blizzard.

After reaching the great forest in the Rocky Mountains, Paul sent Brimstone Bill and Babe on to the Pacific Coast to meet Billy Whiskers and help unload the boat. They finally found the ship outside the entrance to the Golden Gate.

"What's the matter?" shouted Brimstone Bill, "Why don't you come in to shore?"

"I can't!" cried Billy Whiskers through a

large megaphone. "My ship is stuck fast to the bottom of the ocean."

That seemed very queer to Brimstone Bill, for the water was almost a mile deep out in the ocean beyond the Golden Gate. Billy Whiskers rowed ashore and explained. It seems they had made a mistake when they built the ship. The men used new, green lumber and it quickly became water-soaked and the boat started sinking. As soon as the water came up to the edge of the deck, Billy Whiskers would put in to shore and build another deck on top of the first deck.

When that became water-soaked he would build still another deck on top of that. When he finally arrived at the Golden Gate he found he had one hundred and thirty-seven decks on his ship. And all but one of them was under the water!

Of course, with a boat like that, they couldn't go through the Golden Gate, and all the cargo had to be put on rafts and floated ashore. There they loaded everything on the big Blue Ox and were soon back in Paul Bunyan's camp in the Rocky Mountains.

The Mountain That Stood
On Its Head

WHEN Billy Whiskers and his men arrived, Paul Bunyan decided to move further into the mountains. The men wanted to stop and cut the large trees. "No," said Paul, for he had heard of a wonderful white-pine forest that only Indians had ever seen.

Many strange sights they saw as they pushed on through the mountains. There were shovel-tailed beavers that built dams in the streams. Their tails were shaped like shovels and they could build a dam in a few minutes. Hot Biscuit Slim caught six of them and used the beavers to dig holes near the kitchen to bury the prune stones that were left after breakfast.

They saw stiff-legged deer with no joints in their legs. These strange animals could not lie down. They slept standing on their feet, leaning against the trees. They caught several of these by sawing some of the trees almost in two. When the deer would lean against them, the trees would topple over, and so would the deer. Naturally, the deer couldn't get up and were easily captured.

Brimstone Bill caught a sidehill goat. This animal is probably the rarest of all mountain goats. The legs on one side are much shorter than the legs on the other. He travels around the steep sides of the mountain as if he were on level ground. Brimstone Bill made a pet of his sidehill goat and he never got lost or ran away from camp. Because of short legs on one side, he always ran around in a circle when on level ground.

The men also found some sundodgers. These queer birds lay their eggs on the shady side of a mountain. The eggs, instead of being round, are square so they won't roll down the steep mountain sides.

In the center of the wilderness, they came upon the strangest sight they had ever seen. A huge mountain appeared before them. But instead of the peak being in the clouds, it was on the ground. The base of the mountain became wider as it left the ground, like a huge ice-cream cone.

"The Mountain That Stood on Its Head!" cried Paul, as he saw the vast forest of white pines growing down toward the earth from the sides of the mountain. "The Indians told me of it, but said no one could cut the trees because they were growing upside down."

This didn't stop Paul Bunyan, however. He immediately built a camp under the edge of the mountain. Then he called Johnnie Inkslinger to him.

"Here is a new problem for you. How are we going to log off the white-pine trees that are growing upside down from the sides of the mountain?"

Johnnie Inkslinger took off his glasses and thought and thought. He thought of sixty-nine different ways of cutting down the trees but none of them would work. Finally he had Ole the Big Swede build a great cannon and loaded it with gunpowder and heavy iron cannon balls.

When it was ready, they shot the cannon balls through the trunks of the trees, and they dropped upside down to the ground with a loud crash. But the tops of the trees were pointed like arrows, and they plunged into the earth and disappeared from sight. Paul finally had to give the plan up.

They worked all summer without being able to get a single log. Paul was in despair. No task was too large or too difficult for Paul and his men, but they were defeated so far by the Mountain That Stood On Its Head.

It was Tiny Tim, the water boy, who finally thought of a way. "Why not lasso the trees with ropes like the cowboys do?" said Tim, who had read cowboy stories. Paul combed his beard with a young pine tree as he sat thinking about what Tiny Tim had said.

"Not a bad idea!" said Paul.

So they sent to Montana for some cowboys who arrived at the camp with their long lariats. The lariats were ropes the cowboys used to lasso cows and horses. In a short time the air was full of swinging ropes as the cowboys looped them around the tops of the trees.

They tied the lariats to Babe the Blue Ox, and Babe pulled the trees out by the roots. Then the cowboys climbed the mountain, hanging to the upside-down trees by their knees like monkeys, and lassoed other trees.

In a month Paul had logged all the white-pine trees off one side of the mountain. The weight of the trees on the other side caused the mountain to fall over on its side with a great crash that could be heard for miles and miles. The force of the mountain falling started a huge tidal wave on the Pacific Ocean which destroyed sixty fishing villages in Japan.

That is why the geographies no longer show the strange "Mountain That Stood On Its Head."

The Giant Cornstalk

THE Rocky Mountain Country was filled with the largest trees that Paul and his men had ever seen. In fact, everything in the country seemed to grow to tremendous size. Even the mosquitoes were as large as mallard ducks, and the men used chicken wire for mosquito nets.

One day Johnnie Inkslinger sent east for some large imported bumblebees to drive the mosquitoes away. The scheme didn't work out very well. The bumblebees immediately made friends with the mosquitoes and even married them. And the worst of it was, their children were even more terrible than the original mosquitoes, for they had stingers fore and aft and could sting you coming or going!

The whole swarm disappeared one day and settled on a ship loaded with sugar that was anchored in Puget Sound. After they had eaten

89

their fill of the sugar they were too heavy to fly back to land. The entire lot fell in the water and were drowned trying to fly to shore.

Paul decided that this must be very good farming country and started looking around for a good place to raise vegetables for his camp. He came to a beautiful valley with the richest-looking soil he had ever seen.

"That's good soil," said Ole the Big Swede, "but I don't think there is any water in it to make things grow."

Paul took a pickaxe he had with him and drove the point of it in the ground. Water spouted in a great stream a hundred feet high!

"It looks as if there is plenty of water," said Paul. And to this day, that same stream of water still shoots high in the air. They call it Old Faithful Geyser, and you will find it still there in Yellowstone Park.

Paul wanted to test the soil, so he planted a kernel of corn. In five minutes the corn sprouted up through the ground and swiftly grew taller and taller. Soon it was over fifty feet high. Paul called quickly to Ole the Big Swede:

"Climb up and cut off the top of this cornstalk so it will branch out. It is growing altogether too tall!"

Ole climbed the cornstalk and was soon out of sight. And the cornstalk kept growing higher and higher. When Ole tried to slide down the stem to the ground, he found it grew up faster than he could slide down. In order to save Ole, Paul decided the best thing to do was to cut it down at once. Two of his men started sawing, but it grew so fast that it jerked the saw right out of their hands.

He then gave orders for the Seven Axemen to chop it down. They too had to give up, as they never hit the cornstalk twice in the same place. By the time they hit it a second time with their axes, the marks of the first cuts had grown out of sight above their heads.

For two days, they tried to cut the stalk down without result. Paul was afraid Ole might starve to death up on top of the cornstalk, so he sent Brimstone Bill back to camp for his shotgun and some of Hot Biscuit Slim's doughnuts. He finally located Ole with the aid of a spyglass and shot the doughnuts up to him.

About this time the sheriff came up to Paul. He threw back his coat and showed his policeman's star.

"Whose cornstalk is this?" he demanded gruffly.

"It's mine," said Paul.

"Well, it's against the law," said the sheriff, looking very important, "and I order that it be cut down immediately."

"That's exactly what we have been trying to do for two days," said Paul. The sheriff finally went away, as he knew that if anyone could cut that stalk down, it would be Paul Bunyan.

Brimstone Bill suggested that they twist one of Babe's great iron shoes around the base of the cornstalk and choke off the sap so it would quit growing. This was tried and was a success. The stalk quit growing. Paul then ordered the Seven Axemen to chop it down, after shouting to Ole to jump just before it hit the ground.

The cornstalk was so tall by this time that it took fully three hours for it to fall, and Ole had plenty of time to leap to safety as it neared the ground. It fell with such force that it caused cyclones as far away as the Mississippi Valley.

Tiny Tim and the Poisoned Turnips

ONE SUMMER in the Rocky Mountains when Paul had his camp on Tadpole Creek, a big lumberjack walked into the blacksmith shop. Ole and Shot Gunderson were busy at the anvil, punching holes in doughnuts.

"I'm Wildcat Bill, the Bull of the Woods," bellowed the stranger, "and I can whip any man on two feet!"

Ole only laughed and kept on working. "Wait till Paul Bunyan hears about this," he said to Shot Gunderson.

"And who is this Paul Bunyan?" roared the stranger. "I will break him in two with my bare hands!" Paul was walking by and heard this. Paul reached inside and picked him up between two of his fingers and dropped him in the creek to cool him off.

The whole camp roared with laughter as Wildcat Bill slowly waded to shore. Never again did Wildcat Bill call himself the Bull of the Woods, but he hated Paul Bunyan and waited until he could have revenge.

He knew Paul loved Babe the Blue Ox, so one day when everybody was in the woods, he hid some poison in a patch of turnips that Babe loved to eat. He left camp, thinking no one had seen him. However, Tiny Tim was in the next field. He was building a beehive for his two pet bees, Bum and Bill, who made honey for the camp. Tiny Tim saw it all and didn't know what to do!

Soon Babe the Blue Ox returned to camp and went into the turnip field to have his usual lunch of nice fresh turnips. Tiny Tim waved his hat and shouted at Babe, but Tiny Tim was so small and Babe was so large, that the sound never reached his ears.

Tiny Tim then tried to climb up one of Babe's front legs to shout a warning in his ear. He was almost up to Babe's knee, which was about fifteen feet off the ground, when Babe swished his tail and knocked poor little Tim back into the turnips. The ox thought Tiny Tim was a fly or perhaps a mosquito.

"What shall I do?" cried Tiny Tim.

He knew Paul Bunyan would be heartbroken

if Babe ate the poisoned turnips. Finally, he had an idea. So he ran back to the beehive that he had just built. Bum and Bill, his two pet bees, were inside. He closed the door of the beehive and picked up a large stick.

Tiny Tim pounded the top of the beehive with the stick, and the two bees inside buzzed and buzzed, for they were very angry at being disturbed. Tiny Tim pounded the beehive until the bees were good and angry.

"Buzzzzzzzzz!" said Bum, as he flew madly around inside the hive.

"Buzzzzzzzzz!" said Bill, who was just as angry as Bum.

"Now we will see what they will do," said Tiny Tim. So he quickly opened the door of the beehive and hid behind a large cabbage.

Bum and Bill rushed out, mad as hornets. They saw Babe the Blue Ox in the field eating turnips. They flew at Babe in a beeline! Surely Babe must be the one who disturbed their work.

They both stung Babe at the same time! Babe bellowed in fright and ran out of the turnip field. He jumped over the kitchen and knocked down the smokestack. Loads of ashes fell inside and completely covered a fresh batch of hot biscuits the cooks were making.

Babe ran for miles and miles and left huge holes in the ground at every jump.

Paul Bunyan learned how Tiny Tim had kept Babe the Blue Ox from eating the poisoned turnips, and he gave Tim a small axe made of the best steel in the country. He promoted Tiny Tim to axeman and took him out in the woods every day with the men.

Paul also rewarded Bum and Bill, the pet bees. He sent to Norway for the flowers they liked and always planted them near the camp. Bum and Bill forever after had the best of flowers for making their famous honey.

Paul Hunts the Giant Moose

*P*AUL BUNYAN was not only the greatest logger in the country, but he was also a mighty hunter. He could walk for weeks without tiring, and could track down the wildest animal. One day Paul had shot a large grizzly bear. Just for practice, he followed the bear tracks back through the woods and over the mountains to the very spot where the bear was born.

One winter the men discovered huge tracks in the snow near the camp on Tadpole Creek. They thought at first it was Babe, but Babe had not been away from camp all day. They showed Paul the giant tracks in the snow.

"It's the Giant Moose!" cried Paul Bunyan.

No one in the West had ever seen the Giant Moose of the Rockies, although many woodsmen had seen his tracks in the snow. The tracks were so large and so far apart that nobody could follow them.

Paul called for his gun. He said he would follow the Giant Moose and find him if he had to hunt all winter. Bidding farewell to his men, he took with him only Elmer, his famous moose hound, and strode off through the forest.

Elmer was a very queer dog. It seems that one day, an axeman had thrown a sharp double-bitted axe at a tree. It missed the tree and hit Elmer, cutting the dog right in two in the middle. Paul rushed over and quickly sewed the dog back together again, but in the excitement, he sewed the rear part upside down. Elmer soon was as good as ever again, but his two hind legs pointed straight up in the air.

This really wasn't so bad though, because Elmer ran along nicely on his front legs and then when he became tired, he would turn over and run on his hind legs. In that way, he could run for miles and miles without becoming weary.

Night and day Paul followed the tracks of the Giant Moose. Over mountains and across rivers, he followed the giant tracks, but the moose always kept ahead of him.

Far away in Canada, Paul caught a glimpse

of the Giant Moose, drinking at a lake. Before he could draw his gun, the moose leaped over a low range of mountains and was far away.

Paul followed him to Alaska and back again down the Pacific Coast. The Giant Moose was becoming tired. Every day Paul was closer at his heels. To save himself, the Giant Moose dived into Puget Sound and swam swiftly across. Paul plunged in after him. On and on they went far up in the mountains.

It was summer before Paul finally caught sight of him again. His giant antlers were caught in a narrow pass between two mountain ranges. Unable to move, he stood there bellowing with rage. His huge hoofs churned the ground and threw up tons of dirt. He pawed up dirt and rocks until a mountain arose behind him. It is there to this day and they call it Mt. Rainier.

Paul raised his gun and drew careful aim. The Giant Moose struggled in vain. Bang!! The first shot was through the heart. Paul Bunyan had come to the end of the hunt, and the Giant Moose of the Rockies was dead!

The Last Camp of Paul Bunyan

*I*T WAS late in the summer when Paul and his faithful moose hound Elmer started back to Paul's camp on Tadpole Creek. Paul was tired after hunting the Giant Moose. In spite of his great size he could average only forty or fifty miles a day.

One day as he was resting in the Bitter Root Mountains of Idaho, he noticed Elmer sniffing in the air and acting very strange.

"What's the matter, Old Boy?" asked Paul. "Are there grizzly bears in these woods?"

In answer, the moose hound only ran forward and back in front of Paul as if urging his master to continue the homeward journey at once. Every once in awhile he would point his nose toward the sky and growl and whine in terror!

Paul climbed the nearest mountain to investigate. What a sight met his horror-stricken eyes? For miles and miles, as far as he could see, the forest was afire! Great clouds of black smoke rolled upward. Leaping swiftly from treetop to treetop, the angry flames rushed toward Paul!

Paul never thought of himself or the danger. In the center of that raging fire was his camp on Tadpole Creek! What had happened to his men? Where were Tiny Tim and Ole and Johnnie Inkslinger and all his brave crew? Had they perished in the flames?

Without a thought for himself, he ran toward that raging wall of fire. Over rivers and lakes he leaped, and on through the forests, stopping only to soak his great handkerchief in a mountain lake. With this tied over his nose and mouth so that he could breathe more easily, he plunged into the blazing forest fire!

The smoke blinded him, and the fire burned great holes in his leather boots. On he ran through the forest fire that scorched his hands and burned his clothing. It was like a fiery furnace! At times he stumbled and fell and the heat burned his beard to a crisp. Pulling himself to his feet by a mighty effort, he would stagger on.

Soon, he came to the blackened remains of his camp on Tadpole Creek. The great camp that covered so many acres was only a smoldering mass of ashes! The giant griddle that was the pride of Hot Biscuit Slim and all the cooks lay in the center of the ruins. It was bent out of shape by the intense heat. In all that fire-swept country there was no trace of his brave men.

Sadly, and with tears in his eyes, Paul Bunyan gazed over the blackened land that had once been the great forest that he loved so well. His brave crew had disappeared. What had happened to them as the raging forest fire surrounded the camp? Most of all, he missed Babe, his great Blue Ox, who had been his companion on all his many adventures.

Although his feet were blistered with the great heat and his clothing hung in shreds, Paul went back to see if he could find Elmer, his faithful moose hound. By that time, the great forest fire had died out, and all the vast mountain country was covered with blackened stumps.

Paul found Elmer with some loggers on the upper Snake River. The loggers looked at Paul in wonder. "Are you the great Paul Bunyan we have heard so much about? The man who has the largest logging camp in the world?"

"I am Paul Bunyan," he said, "but alas, my

camp has burned, and all my men destroyed in the great fire."

The loggers spoke up:

"Your men are safe. We saw them escape. A great Blue Ox that was a hundred times larger than any ox we had ever seen came through the woods. All the men followed him as he cut a path through the trees with his great hoofs. They built rafts here on the Snake River and floated down into the Oregon Country."

Paul Bunyan cried with joy as he heard the great news! His men were safe! Burned and weary as he was, Paul laughed and shouted with joy. Elmer barked happily by his side.

"What happened to Babe the Blue Ox?" asked Paul.

"The Blue Ox disappeared, after leading the men to safety," said the loggers.

Paul lay down to rest and was soon fast asleep. It was the first night's sleep he had had since the fire. In the morning, a soft wet nose nudged his ear. Then a large rough tongue licked his cheek. It was Babe the Blue Ox who had found his master! The faithful animal had searched far and near until he had found Paul!

The loggers were amazed at the great size of Paul Bunyan and his Blue Ox and the enormous breakfast they ate together. They asked Paul if he were going down into the Oregon Country.

"No," said Paul, "my work is over. My men can join other logging camps in Oregon. I am tired and weary, and my beloved forest is burned to the ground. I am going to take Babe the Blue Ox and go up into the mountains where I can hunt and fish with my faithful dog."

No more do the woods resound with the sharp blows of the Seven Axemen. Tiny Tim is no longer the water boy. Hot Biscuit Slim and Cream Puff Fatty are cooking in other camps in the Oregon woods. Brimstone Bill and Ole the Big Swede were last seen in a logging camp near Bend, Oregon. They passed their later years telling of the brave deeds and mighty exploits of Paul Bunyan and of Babe, his Blue Ox.

Paul Bunyan has disappeared from the woods. Some say he is still roaming the forest of the West. No one has seen him, but the woodsmen say the low rumbling thunder in the mountains on a summer night is Paul Bunyan calling to his faithful ox. Others say that the wind whistling through the treetops is the sound of Paul Bunyan striding through the forests as of old.